For Lila, Eliana, and Asher,
for whom I will always go in there

Imprint

A part of Macmillan Publishing Group, LLC
120 Broadway, New York, NY 10271

About This Book

The art for this book was created in Photoshop. The text was set in Century Gothic, Sofia Soft Pro, and Billy,
and the display type is Animated Gothic Lig. The book was edited by Erin Stein and
designed by Carolyn Bull. The production was supervised by Raymond Ernesto Colón,
and the production editor was Dawn Ryan.

Library of Congress Control Number: 2019949492

ISBN 978-1-250-18949-3 (hardcover)

Our books may be purchased in bulk for promotional, educational, or business use.
Please contact your local bookseller or the Macmillan Corporate and Premium Sales
Department at (800) 221-7945 ext. 5442 or by email at MacmillanSpecialMarkets@macmillan.com.

Imprint logo designed by Amanda Spielman

First edition, 2020

1 3 5 7 9 10 8 6 4 2

mackids.com

If you open doors
that aren't yours,
you might find more
than you bargained for.
What lurks back there?
Lollipops to share?
A mustachioed bear in underwear?
Go ahead, take the dare!

DO NOT GO IN THERE!

written by Ariel Horn

illustrated by Izzy Burton

【Imprint】
MAKE YOUR MARK

New York

Bogart and **Morton** didn't always see eye to eye on things.

Do *not* go in there!

But that gold doorknob is so shiny!
I want to touch it!

There is probably a scary wolf with beady eyes who eats bunnies for supper in there!

But look how RED that door is!
Ooh, what if it's like a scratch 'n sniff sticker
and it smells like candy?

Trust me, do NOT go in there.
There's got to be a wolf behind that door.
There's ALWAYS a scary wolf
in these kinds of stories.

No, no, no.
This is a happy kind of story,
with a happy ending.

I bet there are fireworks and party balloons behind that door!
And robots who are in a robot band!

Do NOT go in there!
Maybe that scary wolf was lonely, so he invited his
evil twin to join him, and they're collecting every fork
in the world, so there are lots of pointy things
in there, and you could get hurt!

Is it like a fork fortress? With a gumdrop castle?
I bet there is a chocolate-syrup moat
with graham cracker boats!

NO, the forks are for the SPACESHIP the wolf and his twin are building. Once they eat all the bunnies on Earth, they will have to look for bunnies on other planets!

Maybe there IS a spaceship
in there! With buttons
that we can press!

No. There are WOLVES! Do you hear me?
THE ARE WOLVES!!!

Not wolves: PUPPIES!

Snuggly, soft, cuddly puppies going into
outer space for the very first time!
With names like Captain Chewy and Mr. Slappy!
With puppy-sized space helmets!

We CANNOT go in there!
The scary wolf and evil twin's spaceship
probably just caught fire, and the fire will
spread if you open the door!

WE CAN MAKE
S'MORES!!!

If the fire spreads, we are all DOOMED!

But if we stop the fire, we are all SAVED!

AND there might be a carnival with those spinning rides that make us dizzy!

Or . . . a magic wand that can make us invisible!

Or a room where we can color all over
the walls with permanent markers!

Let's go in there!!